Nicholas Heller
This Little Piggy

Pictures by
Sonja Lamut

Greenwillow Books, New York

The full-color art was painted on canvas with
egg tempera and oil paints.
The text type is Della Robbia BT.

Text copyright © 1997 by Nicholas Heller
Illustrations copyright © 1997 by Sonja Lamut

Printed in Singapore by Tien Wah Press
First Edition   10 9 8 7 6 5 4 3 2 1

Library of Congress Cataloging-in-Publication Data

Heller, Nicholas.
This little piggy / by Nicholas Heller ; pictures by
Sonja Lamut.
        p.   cm.
Summary: In response to Donald's bedtime request
for "just one more story," his grandmother reaches
for his big toe and elaborates on "This Little Piggy
Went to Market."
ISBN 0-688-14049-1 (trade)
ISBN 0-688-15175-2 (lib. bdg.)
[1. Bedtime—Fiction.   2. Grandmothers—
Fiction.   3. Finger play—Fiction.]   I. Lamut,
Sonja, ill.   II. Title.   PZ7.H37426Th
1997   [E]—dc20   95-976   CIP   AC

For Maxim
—N. H.

For my daughter, Anna
—S. L.

"Just one more story!"
said Donald as his grandmother
reached for the light switch.

"Well . . . all right," she replied, reaching for his big toe instead.

This little piggy
sprang out of bed
and turned off the alarm clock.

He got dressed quickly and prodded
his brother through the quilt.
"Get up!" he said. "It's time to go!"

But nothing happened, so he
shrugged his shoulders, picked
up a large basket, and muttered,
"All right. I'll go by myself."
And he set off to market.

his little piggy kept his head
under the quilt until he heard
the front door slam.

Then he poked his head out,
looked around cautiously,
and slipped out of bed.

"Must have left without me!"
he said. "Well, I don't mind."
He yawned and stretched.

He picked up a magazine
and took an apple out of
the fruit bowl.

"I'll just stay home!" he announced,
and trotted off toward the bathroom
to soak in a nice hot bubble bath.

This little piggy slept on until he was awakened suddenly by a deep growl!

"Oh, my goodness!" he cried, sitting up in bed. "What was that? Why, it's my tummy rumbling." He sighed. "Boy, am I hungry! I wonder what's for breakfast?"

He waddled over to the refrigerator and looked inside. "Hmm, what could this be?" he whispered, lifting a large covered platter off the top shelf. "It says, 'For dinner. . . .'"

"Ah, roast beef! Nobody will miss
just one slice," he assured himself.
"Or two," he added, as he got
himself a plate and a knife and
fork from the cupboard.

He sat down at the table and
was soon so busy eating that
he didn't even hear when . . .

This little piggy stood up on the bed and yawned loudly.

Then he jumped off the bed,

put on his sneakers,

and began his morning exercises.

He did a few deep knee bends
and some jumping jacks.

But when he bent over
to touch his toes,
he noticed his brother
at the table.
"Oh no!" he cried.

He ran over, but it was too late!
His brother was just putting the
last morsel of roast beef into
his mouth!
"Now I'll have none!" wailed
the hungry piggy at the top
of his voice.

"What about the last little piggy, Grandma?" asked Donald.

This little piggy wasn't in bed at all. He had been visiting his grandparents for the weekend, and he had had such a good time that he sang "Whee, whee, whee" all the way home.

And he got there
just in time for bed!